A Gift for GRANDPA

Angela Elwell Hunt • *Illustrated by Terry Julien*

Chariot Books™
David C. Cook Publishing Co.

Chariot Books™ is an imprint of David C. Cook Publishing Co.
David C. Cook Publishing Co., Elgin, Illinois 60120
David C. Cook Publishing Co., Weston, Ontario
Nova Distribution Ltd., Torquay, England

A GIFT FOR GRANDPA
©1991 by Angela Elwell Hunt for text and Terry Julien for illustrations

Designed by Dawn Lauck
First Printing, 1991
Printed in the United States of America
95 94 93 92 91   5 4 3 2 1
Cataloging in Publication Data
Hunt, Angela Elwell
A Gift for Grandpa/by Angela Elwell Hunt
p.   cm.
Summary: Grandma trusts in the Lord to provide the perfect gift for Grandpa's birthday, even
though in the beginning the things she receives are not at all what she had in mind.
ISBN: 1-55513-425-4
[1. Gifts—Fiction. 2. Grandmothers—Fiction.
3. Birthdays—Fiction. 4. Christian life—Fiction.] I. Title.
PZ7.H9115G1 1992   92-15754
[E]—dc20   CIP
AC

For Chet Vanscoy,
whose grandma once wove a watch chain
AEH

To Mom and Dad,
who showed me the beauty of words
and the joy of pictures.
TLJ

Main Street is the busiest road in our
small town, but if you follow it out to where I
live with Grandma and Grandpa, the only
traffic is an occasional passing farmer and the
mail buggy.

Unless it's Saturday. Lots of folks pass our house on Saturday, and today Grandma and I are planning to go to town with them.

"Put on your sturdy shoes," said Grandma. Our old horse died so we'll walk the long way into town after breakfast.

We're on a secret mission. Today is Grandpa's birthday and although he'd like most to have a new horse, Grandma and I only have one dollar. We're going to buy him a chain for his pocket watch.

But during breakfast there was a knock on the door.

Outside stood a woman with her baby and a basket of eggs. "Please, ma'am," the woman said, "I'm on my way to town and I need some money for medicine. Would you like to buy some fresh eggs?"

Grandma pulled our dollar from her purse.

"But what about Grandpa's present?" I whispered.

Grandma smiled. "The Lord always provides."

Grandma gave the dollar to the woman and brought the basket into the kitchen.

Grandma looked at the eggs. "Lord, You know I don't need eggs! I need a watch chain."

There was another knock at Grandma's door.

"Please, madam," said the salesman who stood there, "I've been traveling for days and I'm very hungry. I wonder if I could have something to eat?"

Grandma invited the man to rest on the front porch swing while she scrambled the fresh eggs.

When he had finished eating, the salesman said, "You are so kind I'd like to give you something in return. Please accept three bottles of Smith's Miracle Vitamin Tonic which cures anything from poison ivy to dandruff."

Grandma thanked him as he left, but I wondered what she would do with three bottles of Smith's Miracle Vitamin Tonic. She didn't have poison ivy OR dandruff.

Grandma put the bottles in her apron pocket and sat down on the porch swing. "Lord," she whispered, "You know I don't need Miracle Tonic, I need a watch chain."

A farmer came running up the road. "Help!" he yelled. "My prize pig is dying!"

Grandma and I jumped up and ran to where a fat pig lay gasping for breath in the road.

"I was bringing my pig into town for the fair," explained the farmer, "and she just collapsed. I don't know what to do!"

"I have an idea," said Grandma. She reached for the bottles of Smith's Miracle Vitamin Tonic and poured all three into the pig's mouth.

The pig's eyes blinked and blinked again. Her feet twitched. Then she sprang to her feet and began prancing down the road toward town.

The farmer trotted after his pig and called to us: "Thank you, friends, thank you very much!"

Grandpa came in from the fields for lunch and was surprised to see us. "I thought you two were going shopping for my present today," he said with a twinkle in his eye.

Grandma winked at me. "Plans can change," she said, pulling his ear, "but the Lord always provides."

After lunch, Grandpa went back to the fields. Grandma and I were resting on the porch when we saw the farmer coming from town.

"My pig won a ribbon at the fair," he called to Grandma, "and I've brought you a present."

"A present?" asked Grandma.

"My pig had babies!" exclaimed the farmer. "And I'm giving the whole passel of pigs to you. Pigs are too much trouble. I'm going to raise chickens instead."

Grandma didn't want a passel of pigs, but the farmer insisted and left us with a big prancing pig and three little dancing pigs. The pigs scattered and rooted around in the front yard, probably looking for more Smith's Miracle Vitamin Tonic.

Grandma sighed. "Lord, You know I don't need pigs, I need a watch chain."

A loaded wagon pulled up outside
Grandma's gate and a young couple greeted us.
"Good afternoon. We just bought the farm
down the road and we need to buy some
livestock. Could you tell us where we could get
some fine pigs like yours?"

Grandma smiled. "You can have these pigs," she said, "right now."

The man was surprised. "You'd GIVE them to us?"

"Yes," said Grandma, shooing the pigs toward the gate. "Just put them in your wagon and take them with you."

"We couldn't take them without giving something in return," said the woman. "Would you accept five quilts in exchange for the pigs?"

"Certainly," said Grandma, eager to be rid of the messy pigs. "Just take these pigs away."

Grandma and I sat in the front porch swing with the stack of quilts between us. We were exhausted. "Lord," Grandma said, looking up at the sky, "You know I don't need five quilts, I need a watch chain."

Just then a new buggy with a team of snappy horses pulled up outside our gate. "Grandma Jones," called Mrs. Thomas, the manager of the town hotel, "I have a problem and I hope you can help."

"What can I do for you?" asked Grandma.

"It's supposed to be cold tonight, and the hotel furnace is broken. Do you have a small kerosene stove I can borrow?"

"I don't have a stove, but I have extra quilts I'll give you," said Grandma, pointing to the quilts. "Is five enough?"

"What a wonderful idea," answered Mrs. Thomas. "But I simply couldn't take such beautiful quilts without doing something for you."

She thought a moment. "You know, it is so much trouble to feed and take care of two horses. I'd be much better off with just one. Would you consider taking one of my horses in trade? You'd be doing me a tremendous favor."

Grandma nodded and placed the quilts in Mrs. Thomas's arms. "Whatever you think best, Mrs. Thomas."

As Mrs. Thomas left, Grandma walked over to the handsome horse now tied to our fence. She patted his neck and said, "Lord, I know we needed a horse. But I wanted a watch chain."

Then I smiled. "Wait here, Grandma. I'll be right back!" I ran into the house and brought out Grandma's sewing basket.

Grandma watched as I measured ten inches of the horse's long, silky tail. SNIP went the scissors.

The birthday horse waited outside for Grandpa and we took the silky horsehair into the house. Grandma helped me braid it into the most beautiful watch chain we had ever seen. Then we wrapped Grandpa's gift and waited for him to come home.